Flash Digest

April 2025

Edited by
Terrie Leigh Relf

THE STAFF OF FLASH DIGEST

EDITOR: Terrie Leigh Relf
WEBMASTER: H. David Blalock
COVER GODDESSES: Laura Givens; Marcia A. Borell

Cover art "Jupiter's Eye" by Richard E. Schell
Cover design by Laura Givens

Vol. II, No.2   March 2025

Flash Digest is published four times a year on the 1st days of January, April, July, and October in the United States of America by Hiraeth Publishing, P.O. Box 1248, Tularosa, NM, 88352. Copyright 2025 by Hiraeth Publishing. All rights revert to authors and artists upon publication except as noted in selected individual contracts. Nothing may be reproduced in whole or in part without written permission from the authors and artists. Any similarity between places and persons mentioned in the fiction or semi-fiction and real places or persons living or dead is coincidental. Writers and artists guidelines are available online at www.hiraethsffh.com. Guidelines are also available upon request from Hiraeth Publishing, P.O. Box 1248, Tularosa, NM, 88352, if request is accompanied by a self-addressed *10 envelope with a first-class US stamp.

Contents

Stories

12	The Witch Across the Street by Vincent Baverso
19	Pont Perilous by Maureen Bowden
28	Athan & Ariel by Tom Duke
36	Don't Talk About the Birds by S.D. Bullard
42	Red River Pawn by Heather Santo
46	Achievable Goals by Jamie Lackey
50	Gate by Jason Eisenmenger
54	The Hungry Forest by Stephen W. Chappell

Illustrations

18	Forest Creature in Spiderweb Outfit by Sandy DeLuca
25	Crowded by April Lefleur

Who?

60	Who's Who

**THERE'S A SALE GOING ON!!!
IT'S STILL GOING ON!!!**

BUY ALL THE BOOKS YOU WANT AND USE THIS 20% DISCOUNT CODE: BOOKS2024

THIS DISCOUNT CAN BE USED AS MANY TIMES AS YOU WISH, SO TAKE ADVANTAGE OF IT!

GO TO OUR SHOP AT WWW.HIRAETHSFFH.COM

NO MASKS, NO WAITING, AND WE NEVER CLOSE!

A Little Help, Please

In the world of the small indie press we fight a never-ending battle for attention to our work, as writers and in publishing. Here's an example: big publishers [you know who they are] have gobs of $$$ that they can devote to advertising and marketing. Here at Hiraeth Publishing, our advertising budget consists of the deposits for whatever soda bottles and aluminum cans we can find alongside the highways. Anti-littering laws make our task even more difficult . . . ☺

That's where YOU come in. YOU are our best promoter. YOU are the one who can tell others about us. Just send 'em to our website, tell them about our store. That's all. Just that.

Of course, we don't mind if you talk us up. We're pretty good, you know. We have some award-winning and award-nominated writers and artists, plus other voices well-deserving to be heard [not everyone wins awards, right?] but our publications are read-worthy nevertheless.

That number once again is:
www.hiraethsffh.com

Friend us on Facebook at Hiraeth Publishing
Follow us on Twitter at @HiraethPublish1

The Sisterhood of the Blood Moon
By Terrie Leigh Relf

For thousands of Earth years, the Transgalactic Consortium has had an invested interest in this planet and its inhabitants, the Haurans. While the Sisterhood of the Blood Moon and the Guardians work together with the Consortium and Haurans to restore balance to the universe, the Blood Moon is fast approaching. The power of this moon reveals untold secrets . . . including the sacred covenant with the Mora Spiders. There is an ancient pact that continues to be honored – but at what cost and for whose purpose?

The world may come to an end. But will there be a chance for a new beginning? And if so, where?

Type: Novel – science fiction/fantasy
Cover price: $14.95
ISBN: 9781087929927

Ordering link:
Print Edition:
https://www.hiraethsffh.com/product-page/sisterhood-of-the-blood-moon-by-terrie-leigh-relf

The Saint and the Demon

By t.santitoro & Ron Sparks

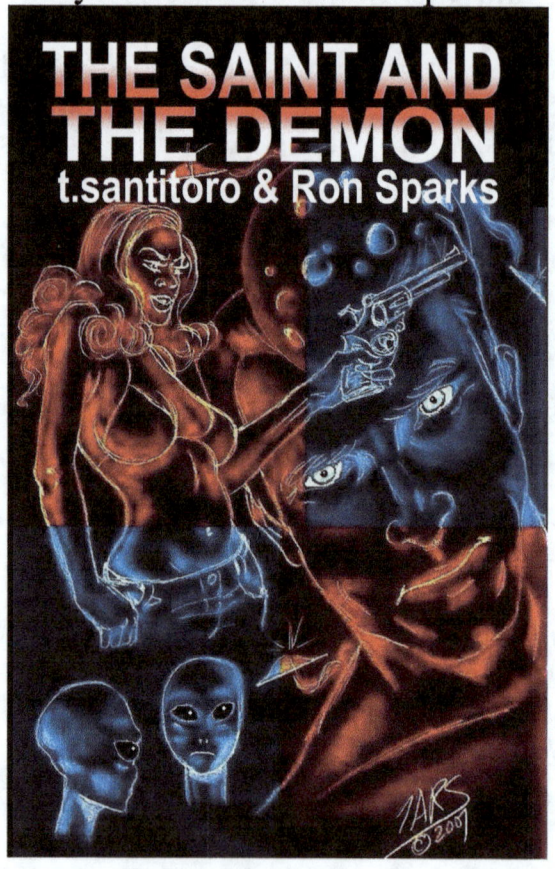

In the not-to-distant future, a young reporter reluctantly agrees to interview a senile old man in the heart of the Florida Everglades. In the humid, swampy environment, the reporter is sure that there can be no story of substance here, but the old man reveals that, in the past, his love was so strong and so passionate for a woman that he stopped at nothing to get her back when the forces of war tore them apart. He became a hero and a coward, a lover and a fighter . . . a saint and a devil. In his quest to rescue the woman he loved, he became something that she could no longer love.

Into the middle of this personal ordeal tumbles Cutter, a man from another world, sent to Earth to establish a breeding mission for his endangered race. He falls in love with an Earth woman, and must defend not only her, but also the future of his own people. The object of his alien affections, an innocent young woman named Angel, finds herself suddenly thrust into a world of aliens and intrigue, and of a love that has far more dangerous consequences than she could possibly have imagined.

Ordering Link:
Print ($13.95): https://www.hiraethsffh.com/product-page/saint-and-the-demon-by-t-santitoro-and-ron-sparks
PDF ($4.99): https://www.hiraethsffh.com/product-page/saint-the-demon-by-t-santitoro-ron-sparks
ePub ($4.99): https://www.hiraethsffh.com/product-page/saint-amp-the-demon-by-t-santitoro-amp-ron-sparks

The Gifted
By Tyree Campbell

DEDICATED TO THE MEMORY OF MELISSA MEAD

The year is 2045. Earth's societies have fallen apart for various reasons—economic, social, political, disease. To live, people began to loot, kill each other, and generally get by from day to day. In the latter stages of this deterioration, fear of disease caused immunizations to be rushed into production without proper testing. Some parents soon discovered that the children born were deformed in some way: flippers for hands and/or feet, missing organs, scales for skin, etc.

In addition to flippered hands and feet, Wendy Meade was gifted with some psi abilities that enabled her to talk with animals and with people. Now an adult woman, she scrapes by in a woods above a bay on the coast of southern Oregon, where there is an abandoned town where food is still available in convenience stores. She supplements this with shellfish from the bay. Such is her life.

Until one day she discovers that she can telepath with animals and people. A small community begins to form around her. Now, if possible, she has to use her powers to protect them from marauders.

Type: Post-Apocalyptic Novel
Ordering links:
Print: https://www.hiraethsffh.com/product-page/gifted-by-tyree-campbell
ePub: https://www.hiraethsffh.com/product-page/gifted-by-tyree-campbell-1
PDF: https://www.hiraethsffh.com/product-page/gifted-by-tyree-campbell-2

The Witch Across the Street
Vincent Baverso

You see the house from across the street, bent and broken down the middle like an overworked horse. The roof is buckling and shingles peel like shedding dragon scales. The house is black, but never painted nor meant to be that color. The stonework absorbed the soot and exhaust from so many years living by a busy street.

A tall hedge blocks most of the house from the street but you see movement at one of the windows. A large black cat parts the sun-scorched drapes to lay on the windowsill. The cat is staring into the hedge, waiting for a squirrel or mouse to skitter across its path. The cat licks its paw, watches, and waits.

As you travel around the back of the house, you see a wrought iron fence standing sentinel like a prison cell. The hedge grows behind the fence, but there are parts that have sprouted through the black iron bars, entangling tendrils.

From the crumbling sandstone foundation, you determine that the house was built before 1900. Easily the oldest home in the neighborhood, as others like it deteriorated with time. Some of the neighborhood kids whisper that the old woman who lives there is the original owner. She is a witch who steals children and eats them to gain their youth. But neighborhood kids will always whisper rumors; that doesn't mean they're always true.

You hear the latch of the deadbolt. She's coming! You scuttle away from her property, heart pounding.

You see her from across the street. Ms. Gwidden is an arthritic, hunchbacked, wrinkled old woman. When she talks, it's to your chest or feet, as she is unable to straighten her back to look in your eyes. Her nose consumes at least half of her face, a hooked, warty, gourd that refuses to stop growing. Her hair sprouts in bristly, gray tufts, covered by a black shawl. Her rheumatic fingers end in long, unpainted nails with dirt embedded under the yellow claws.

She looks up the street, turning her whole body, stiff as the Tin Woodsman. She looks down the street, and you pray she doesn't notice you as she surveys the entirety of the neighborhood. Her hand glides over some plants in a planter next to the front door. Worthless vegetation. She plucks some of them in a single, swift motion. She doesn't struggle to harvest the herbs as her crippled hands would imply. She returns inside, the knocker knocks a single time as it bounces from her slamming the door.

You now slip a little closer to the house across the street. You climb up the crumbling front steps, overgrown moss holding most of the concrete in place. You examine the planter next to the front door. As suspected, the plants are unremarkable, commonplace weeds. The stems, cleanly cut, as if by knife instead of hand.

This close to the door you hear the creak of floorboards, and your heart leaps into your throat. But the footsteps are moving away from you. By the time your pulse slows to normal, you hear the backdoor open with a squeal of rusty hinges.

You work your way around to the back of the house. You catch glimpses of her black dress and shawl through the foliage of the hedge.

Do you think she'll notice if you part some of the foliage? Do you think she'll see?

You separate some of the branches and you clearly see her yard for the first time. The hanging gardens of Babylon, the great botanical conservatories in Padua, Italy, the gardens of Versailles; none compare to what you see before you.

Beautiful and intricate stonework adorns the entirety of the backyard. Raised planters form the boundaries for paths lined with colorful flowers. Snaking vines follow the mortar joints in the stonework and grow like odd, angular snakes.

You see her with a handful of plants and herbs harvested from her gardens. She sits with a mortar and pestle, grinding the plants to a green, pulpy mash. She is facing you, but her head and eyes are pointing down, a product of her crooked back. She dips two fingers into the green mash like a baker tasting cake icing. She greedily licks the milled plant life from her thick and fungus coated nails like a stranded survivor finding food for the first time in days.

Her cat meows.

She sits straighter, her back creaking like an old leather sofa. She is no longer a hunched and shriveled woman. She looks to grow a foot in height. She lifts her head, rubbing the stiffness in her neck. You see her face, no longer the wrinkled and hook-nosed visage, but beautiful. A young woman sits in the gardens, draped in the old crone's clothes. The woman's hair is long and black and flows to her waist. Her eyes angle up at the corners, a natural feature that most women try to emulate with eyeliner. Her nose still holds a slight crook, but carries an air of Mediterranean grace.

She straightens. She stands, without the help of her cane to balance. Her eyes raise to stare at the small section of parted hedge, and her eyes meet yours. An arctic blast gusts down your collar and chills your spine. Paralysis takes you and you cannot move. You want to run, want to flee to the safety of your house across the street.

"Come child, enter my garden," she says, but her mouth never moves. The gate, overgrown with hedge and vines, opens with a creak.

Inside, the gardens are even more beautiful. Like crossing into another plane of existence, unfathomable beauty.

"Now child, as you see, I have many plants here. I have plants for illness, herbs for a younger appearance, and of course, something special for snooping, little children. She hands you a dandelion puff and tells you to make a wish. You wish to be home safe. Rarely do wishes ever come true. But this is a witch's garden, hopefully there is some truth to her magic.

You feel a long and diseased fingernail caress your face. Ms. Gwidden has returned to her ancient self. You close your eyes and blow.

The Red Foil
By t.santitoro

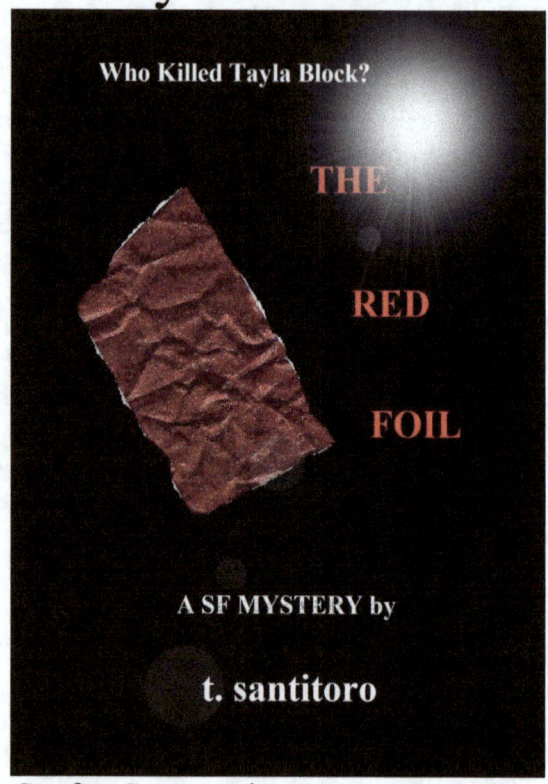

When Soefee Sparrow's roommate and ex-lover, Tayla Block, goes missing aboard a space mining station, Sparrow—a rocket-horse jockey—suddenly finds herself under suspicion of murder.

Despite the mining company's main source of income—megatons of industrial minerals and gem stones—no one but Soefee seems to be searching for their leading geologist.

Were gemstones being stolen from the mining company? Did it have anything to do with Block's disappearance? Why was everyone being so tight-lipped?

What happened to Tayla Block, and why wasn't anything being done to find her?

Enter Jicob Elfrendini, an undercover agent for IBCP, a division of Law Enforcement employed to ensure against the theft of valuable gems. But Elfrendini has secrets of his own.

And then a woman's dead body is found at the bottom of a mine shaft and, together, Soefee and Jicob must work to find out who killed Tayla Block—

--and WHY?

Print: https://www.hiraethsffh.com/product-page/red-foil-by-t-santitoro
ePub: https://www.hiraethsffh.com/product-page/red-foil-by-t-santitoro-2
PDF: https://www.hiraethsffh.com/product-page/red-foil-by-t-santitoro-1

Forest Creature in Spiderweb Outfit
Sandy DeLuca

Pont Perilous
Maureen Bowden

On a warm September day, I sat on the banks of the River Brue, with the sun on my back and birdsong easing my mind. I picked up three pebbles from the riverbank. Resting them in the palm of my hand, I imagined that they were the gallstones that had been gnawing at my gut, reducing me to a howling wraith. In two days' time, they'd be cut out of me. That would be one less embuggerance blighting my existence, leaving me with the remaining one, my hateful husband, till death us do part. I flung the pebbles into the water, with a silent wish that I could do the same to him. The ripples spread. The outer one reached the foot of Pomparles Bridge stretching across the river. A figure was leaning over the side, watching me.

He shuffled towards me like a shy five-year-old. "Can I sit by 19ccu?"

"Are you Welsh?" I said.

"I'm a Celt, so it's sorta the same thing, see." He was tall and skinny, with enough ginger curls to stuff a cushion. His eyes were green as garden peas, his tee shirt and combat pants were black, and his skin had what my husband's probation officer would have called prison pallor. I'd never met anyone like this anaemic mop-top before, but somehow he seemed like an essential component of the location.

I patted the ground and he flopped down beside me, offering his hand. "Gwynn's the name."

I shook it. "Hello, Gwynn. I'm Melanie."

"Alright Mel. What's 19ccurring'?"

"Nothing much: spending the weekend in Glastonbury, relaxing, chucking stones into the river."

"Tidy." He placed his finger on my wedding ring. "Oh, there's something you ain't tellin'. Seems to me you wanted to chuck this in too, like; and the fly-bitten codpiece who gave it to you."

"Maybe I did, but I'm stuck with him. I made a vow."

"So did he, but he does what he likes, isn't it?"

"Good guess," I said, "but it's not the vow I made to him that I have to keep. It's the one I made to myself when I was a child." I had no idea why I was off-loading my troubles onto a gangly Celt I'd known for two minutes, but he seemed to drag the words out of me. "I was ten years old when my mother ran off with a Bruce Willis look-alike from Milton Keynes. My dad and I never saw her again. She broke her vow, and I swore that I'd never do that, so I'm stuck."

"Get over yourself, Mel," he said. "I gets it. The vows we makes to ourselves locks us up and bolts the door, but it's only till you die."

"Is that supposed to make me feel better?"

"It should. There's always a way out, look you. See that bridge by 20ccu?"

"What about it?"

"It's the Pont Perilous. Back in the day, Sir Galahad and Sir Percival crossed it looking for the Holy Grail."

"Did they find it?"

Gal did. He was a bit too goodie-goodie for me, but Percy was a crackin' boyo. Never found the Grail but he had a lotta fun tryin,' see?"

"Not really. What's it got to do with me?"

"The Pont Perilous leads to what you're looking for. Apart from Grail seekers, folk don't cross until it's time for them to go to the Otherworld, mind, and they can't do that until they're dead."

"What would I find if I crossed it now?"

"The road to the local shoe factory. Useful, but I won't lie to you; it's not in the same league as the Holy Grail."

"Unless you're desperate for a pair of shoes."

"Fair point, Mel. I'll grant you that, but I'm here to tell you that whatever you're desperate for the bridge is waiting for you when you're ready."

His ramblings about the Grail and the Otherworld were making me uneasy. "Who are you?" I said.

"Gwynn ap Nudd." He smiled, and looked into my eyes. They grew heavy. The gurgle of the river transformed into a long-forgotten lullaby, and I drifted into sleep.

When I awoke, a late afternoon chill was in the air and Gwynn had gone. I shivered, scrambled to my feet, and retraced my steps, back across Wearyall Hill, into Glastonbury.

On the High Street I wandered into the Vesica Piscis Bookshop and browsed through the shelves. *Glastonbury Legends* caught my eye. I found "Gwynn ap Nudd" in the index, turned to the appropriate page, and read:

"If you fall asleep on Glastonbury Tor, Gwynn ap Nudd, ruler of the Otherworld will steal your soul. We all visit the Land of Nudd in our dreams but if King Gwynn takes you he doesn't bring you back."

I laughed, feeling lucky not to have met him on the Tor. I put the book back on the shelf. That was enough hippy-trippy nonsense for one day.

I returned to the guesthouse I'd booked for the weekend, ate a light evening meal that my afflicted digestive system could tolerate, and retreated to my room to spend another Saturday night alone.

I awoke to a grey September morning. Rain splattered the window and autumn was sneaking up on summer. I packed, checked out and drove home.

I opened my front door and heard the sounds of human activity upstairs. The fly-bitten codpiece was, no doubt, cavorting in the bedroom with his latest squeeze, Gollum in a frock. I needed to be somewhere else: anywhere else. Ignoring the racket I crept into my own bedroom, crawled into bed and fell asleep.

On Monday morning, I drove to the hospital. The surgeon said, "The procedure is straightforward keyhole surgery, Melanie. We make a small incision and pull out your gall bladder. You'll have a tiny scar that will look like a dimple when it heals. Any questions?"

"Are there risks?" I asked.

"There are always risks," he said, "but it's a very common operation and you're in good hands. Don't worry."

After a series of questionnaires, blood tests, poking and prodding, I was at last, on a trolley parked next to a tropical fish tank that was presumably meant to induce inner serenity. The theatre nurse stuck a needle in my arm and told me to count backwards from ten. I reached eight before passing into oblivion.

I was floating in the void when I heard a voice, from a long way off, say, "She's arrested," and I was looking down at my body on the operating table. The doctors clustered around me. I could sense their agitation.

A whirlpool of light sucked me in, spun me around and dumped me at the foot of Wearyall Hill, on the banks of the River Brue. The sun was setting in a blue and gold sky, staining the clouds pink, and I caught the twilight scent of honeysuckle.

Gwynn was sitting on the bridge, dangling his stick-thin legs over the side. He waved, and called to me, "Oh, Mel. What's 23ccurring'?"

"I think I'm dead."

"Tidy." He bounded towards me. "Is you ready to cross the bridge, now?"

"What will I find on the other side?" I said.

"It depends what you expect to find, like."

"But it won't be a shoe factory?"

He grinned. "Not unless you're desperate for a pair of shoes."

I felt calm, and more content than I had in years. "Let's do it."

"Crackin'." He took my hand, but as he led me forward I felt a jolt in my chest. The air grew misty, the scene faded, and I was back in the operating theatre.

I screamed, "No," hurled myself through the bright spiral, and was once again standing with Gwynn at the foot of the bridge. "What happened?" I said.

"Where did you die, Mel?"

"In hospital. I was having my gall bladder removed."

"They're trying to pull you back. Is you up for it?"

"What do I have to go back for? I'm miserable, lonely and tied by my own stubbornness to a man I despise."

"You needs a good kickin', girl. The vow was 'Till death us do part,' see? You kept it till you died. You does whatever you wants now. The bridge will still be there when you've done it."

My biggest embuggerance drained away. "You're right, Gwynn. I have a life to live. The Otherworld can wait. See you in about fifty years' time."

"Tidy."

I fell back into my unconscious body and when I awoke, I was ready to start living.

Whispers of Magic
By Maureen Bowden

Legends and unusual characters abound in England, where you never know who or what you might meet in the forests. Maureen Bowden introduces you to them in these stories of magic and misdirection...and invites you to stay.

Maureen Bowden is a Liverpudlian, living with her musician husband in North Wales. In addition to stories, she also writes song lyrics, mostly comic political satire, set to traditional melodies. She loves her family and friends, rock 'n' roll, Shakespeare, and cats.

https://www.hiraethsffh.com/product-page/whispers-of-magic

Crowded
April Lefleur

Secrets of the Nether Moor
By Allison Tebo

Charlotte Morrison is a shy squire's daughter who is better suited to stitchery than spells. But when she discovers that her beloved brother is the author behind a series of revolutionary pamphlets decrying their oppressive government, her life changes overnight.

With the people's hero under arrest, Charlotte cannot depend on the legendary Jack O'Lantern to save her brother—so she takes matters into her own hands by boarding the infamous night coach through the Nether Moor: a place haunted by aberrations and monsters.

But danger lurks within the carriage as well as without. Charlotte is following Major Pegg, the cruel official carrying the papers that will bring about her brother's arrest. If she ever hopes to save her brother, Charlotte must steal the papers before they reach the Crossroads.

Armed with nothing but a spell bomb and desperation, Charlotte cannot rely on legends. It is up to her to save her brother and be her own kind of hero.

Secrets of the Nether Moor is an adventure set in an alternate Georgian England, featuring the outlaws that haunt the forgotten places and the heroes that can be found in the most ordinary hearts.

Print $9.95: www.hiraethsffh.com/product-page/secrets-of-the-nether-moor-by-allisontebo
ePub $2.99: www.hiraethsffh.com/product-page/secrets-of-the-nether-moor-by-allison-tebo-1
PDF $2.99: www.hiraethsffh.com/product-page/secrets-of-the-nether-moor-by-allison-tebo

Athan & Ariel
Tom Duke

Athan reached across the glass counter and accepted his lip balm purchase from the cosmetics department sales associate. She looked mid-twenties, wearing round platinum-rimmed glasses and black hair styled in an asymmetrical pixie cut with purple highlights that cascaded over the right side of her forehead like a dark waterfall. Her neck —slender and perfect as a Venetian vase—was decorated with a small tattoo near the carotid artery that appeared to be a raven taking flight. Fascinating. She was quite attractive in a punk yet bookish way.

He had just entered the store from the mall's outdoor promenade, where he'd spent the past hour pretending to be one of the shoppers as he strolled among them, pausing to peer through store fronts, using the reflection from the windows to see if his broad-shouldered, narrow-hipped, six-foot-two frame garnered any interest. But the few looks he'd received were from individuals attached to small groups—risky. So he had decided to ditch the mall scene and try some nightclubs, and on his walk back to the parking structure, had cut through the big store. That's when he spotted her, patrolling the isles and adjusting displays while waiting for closing.

The area surrounding the cosmetics department was quiet, as the store's few remaining shoppers moved toward checkout registers in other departments. Even under the bright store lights, Athan felt isolated; he and the young sales associate—only the glass counter between them—virtually alone.

During the exchange he'd caressed her thumb with his index finger. Would she think it was an accident or a come-on? Was he creep or charmer? Her eyes searched his for an answer as he applied some balm to his lips. In that moment, his sensual charm slipped into her subconscious, and her wariness dissipated. The whispering scent of her female pheromones activated his salivary glands. "Thank you," he said, breaking the spell, "I think I'm addicted to this stuff. Left mine at home. Your kindness has surely saved my evening."

Athan certainly was charming, even enchanting. He attracted women of all ages—and not just women. But his allure had deeper roots; he had something humans subconsciously wanted. They had something he needed.

He used a beverage analogy to describe his tastes: women, in general, were mostly like wine; men, more like whiskey. He knew the analogy was a cliché, but he also knew it as fact.

Because he tasted it.

She looked at him quizzically. "Do I know you?"

"Of course, Ariel." Athan smiled, flashing perfect teeth. "I am he who seeks lip balm just before store closing."

A short laugh escaped her. She flicked her name tag with her index finger. "I hate this thing," she complained. "It makes me feel . . . "

"Insignificant?"

"Exactly. And this job is a career path to death-by-boredom."

"What are you doing about it?"

"I'm waiting."

"Those who wait are always late."

"That's not true."

"It is, and you know it."

"I'm waiting for the right moment."

"A future moment is an idea, not a reality."

"It *can* be."

"Let us go then, you and I . . ."

"Hey, I know that." She brightened. "T.S. Eliot. 'The Love Song of J. Alfred Profrock'. I was *so* mesmerized by that poem in college literature. It's like a waking dream."

"Some dreams, waking or not, are more than just dreams."

"What does that mean?"

"There's more to existence than dreams and reality. There are places In-Between."

"Yes . . . places In-Between. I never thought of it like that."

"You've experienced the In-Between?"

Ariel hesitated. He sensed her struggling with an old secret, one he could tell haunted her. He probed. "Something you are uncomfortable discussing?"

"I was six," her voice wavered, "I woke in the middle of the night, thought I heard . . . or sensed something in the house, in my mom's room."

"Did you see anything?"

"I'm not sure if I was awake or dreaming or . . . somewhere In-Between. But the air above my mom seemed alive, agitated . . . doing something to her. She was moaning in her sleep. I couldn't tell if she was in pain or pleasure. I tried to call out to her, but my mouth wouldn't work. I wanted to go to her, but . . . my legs . . ."

Ariel peered down through the glass counter at the collection of cosmetics in the case below. He saw her image, like the ghost of a lost girl, captured in the glass. She barely got the next part out. "Then it looked at me. I couldn't see it, but I *felt* its stare boring into me, making my insides churn." She raised her head and met Athan's eyes. "It wanted me, too."

A sudden electrical charge of recognition shot down Athan's spine and settled in his groin.

He knew her.

Nearly two decades ago.

She was only six . . .

. . . that night he sipped of her mother.

Could she sense who he was? Impossible. "I gather your mom was all right?"

"I must have blacked out because that's all I remember," said Ariel, still staring downward. "The next morning, I went to mom's room. She was tired and weak, had chills and a headache. I thought maybe she'd caught some bug. I wanted to tell her about the *thing*, but I didn't know how. So I pretended it was only a dream and tried to forget about it. But I couldn't. Even though mom got better physically she never quite regained her old vibrant self. I mean, she was okay, but it was as if her spirit was slowly fading away.

"Last year she was diagnosed with dementia. She was only fifty and went downhill fast. I had to put her in an assisted living facility. It wasn't long before she could no longer recognize me. She passed a month ago, but what's strange is I was visiting her a few days earlier, and she took my hand and told me she loved me and that she missed me, as if she was already gone and was waiting for me. I almost lost it right then."

"I'm sorry, Ariel," said Athan, surprised by his sympathetic tone. "At least you had a chance to say goodbye. But she's gone now, and you must move on for your own sake."

Her voice was that of the six year old. "It's been coming to my bedroom almost every night since she passed."

Athan was taken aback. He had never imagined being confronted by the psychic leftovers from one of his of his feedings. She was clearly standing near a cliff's edge, the weight of guilt, loss, and despair dragging her ever closer. "It's not real," he finally offered, "just a remnant from your childhood trauma, a dark echo from the In-Between. It can't hurt you."

"No? But it seems so real. I always wake up, or think I'm awake, and I can feel it hovering over me. But it's different, changed, as if part of my mom is in there also, trying to reach out to me. But I can't actually see or hear anything. I can only feel it . . . wanting."

Athan caught himself nodding . . . wanting.

"I wish I'd had the courage to enter my mom's room that night and chase the thing away. If I wasn't such a coward, maybe she'd still be here." Her eyes fell back to the counter again, as her voice trailed off. "I've never even told this to anyone before."

"You *were* brave," said Athan, "only a child, and that little girl needs your compassion." His voice softened, "you faced something that, even as an adult, you're still struggling to comprehend. Yet you made a difference. Just being there at that moment probably saved your mom's life. And all these years later, here you are, still fighting thorough it, finally beginning to unburden yourself of undeserved guilt."

Arial stirred, conflict shadowing her face, as if she were battling to re-interpret her memories.

Athan turned to leave, the nightclub run still on. "Take care, Ariel. Don't fear the In-Between; it's no more dangerous than dreams or reality."

She looked up with a smile that seemed unsure of itself. But what else did he see, a glimmer of hope?

I could sip of her tonight, Athan mused as he strode toward the store's exit, but a rare twang of empathy and compassion had vibrated into his consciousness.

Besides, tonight he had a taste for whiskey.

Living Bad Dreams
By Denise Hatfield

When dreams come alive, there's no telling where they will lead. Everything changes when you realize that, dream or no dream, you're going to die. What do you do then?

Ordering Link:
Print: https://www.hiraethsffh.com/product-page/living-bad-dreams-by-denise-hatfield-1

ePub: https://www.hiraethsffh.com/product-page/living-bad-dreams-by-denise-hatfield-2
PDF: https://www.hiraethsffh.com/product-page/living-bad-dreams-by-denise-hatfield

Heir Apparent
Tyree Campbell

Answering a distress call, March and Myrrha find a young woman who has deliberately been marooned on an uninhabited world. She claims to be Hoya Palologa, heir to the Palologa throne on Wanderby. But there is already a Hoya who has been invested as the heir apparent to that throne. Myrrha believes the claim of the Hoya she and March have encountered. Thus begins a journey to establish the succession, a journey made far more perilous because Hoya not only claims the throne, but is also a sinister personage with several crimes on her resume.

March and Myrrha find themselves embroiled in internal politics on Wanderby, where the slightest wrong move can get them killed. The rulers on that world are oblivious to the subtle machinations of their underlings, one of whom has created a lookalike but false Hoya. Which one is which? And will death take the real one before March and Myrrha can stop it?

Type: Novel – science fiction

Ordering Links:
Print: https://www.hiraethsffh.com/product-page/heir-apparent-by-tyree-campbell
PDF: https://www.hiraethsffh.com/product-page/heir-apparent-by-tyree-campbell-2
ePub: https://www.hiraethsffh.com/product-page/heir-apparent-by-tyree-campbell-1

Don't Talk About the Birds
S.D. Bullard

It's been three weeks since the birds disappeared. People don't seem to notice. I'm sure they noticed birds when they were around, noticed but didn't really think about it. But now? No one seems to realize they're gone. All of them. At least all of them around here. But no one notices. Except me.

"You said she can't communicate?" The man is speaking. A detective. Detective Herring. He smells like soap, bar soap, not the liquid kind, and the same chewing tobacco my uncle Garth uses. He missed a button on his blue shirt and the room we're in is too bright and too small and I wish someone would understand about the birds.

"No," Mom says. "No, I said she can't talk. She can communicate. It can just be tricky to understand sometimes."

"Uh huh," Detective Herring says. "You think she comprehends what we're saying?"

Of course I do, I just wish we weren't in such a small space because in here his voice feels too loud, too loud and too big and too tight in my ears. I rock, just a little, forward and back. It helps settle the words and the tightness.

"Oh yes," Mom says. "Yes, she's very smart. Her doctor describes it like a one-way mirror. Everything goes in, it's just hard for her to put anything back out."

I feel Detective Herring looking at me, but I don't look back. I don't like faces. They change too much, and I don't understand them. Instead, I glance to my left, to the big mirror. I wonder if that's a one-way mirror. They always have them on police shows and Detective Herring is a police. But there's a smudge on the mirror and it's shaped kind of like a bird and I look away and rock a little more.

"Why is she doing that?"

"It helps her calm herself."

Detective Herring sighs. I know a sigh is supposed to mean frustration. Maybe he doesn't like this room either.

"I'm not sure how I'm supposed to make this work."

"Here," Mom says, and she pulls out my tablet, the one with all the prerecorded words and phrases on it. She navigates to the "yes/no" button page and slides the tablet in front of me. "If you can keep the questions to yes or no answers that might work best."

"Okay." Detective Herring scoots a little closer to the table. I wish he wouldn't. I don't like people near me, even if they are across the table.

"Lottie, listen to the detective now. I want you to answer his questions."

"Lottie." Detective Herring taps the table a few times, taps on some pictures that sit on the table in front of him. "Do you know Elinor Markavich?"

"Miss Ellie," Mom adds softly.

Of course I know Miss Ellie. She's been my speech therapist since I was two. I pull the tablet closer to me and tap until I find the button I want.

"*Birds*," the prerecorded voice says.

"Sorry," Mom says. "She really likes watching birds. Lottie, I'll take you to see the birds when we're done here. You need to answer Detective Herring's questions right now."

How is she going to take me to see something that isn't there?

"Do you know Miss Ellie?" Detective Herring asks again.

I swipe back to the "Yes" button and hit it. Why is he asking me about Miss Ellie? She can't do anything to help. Not anymore. She's gone. Just like the birds.

"Did you see Miss Ellie three weeks ago, on Friday afternoon?"

"*Yes.*" My appointments were always Friday afternoon.

"Were you at Davidson Park?"

I like the park. There are lots of birds around. Or there used to be. That's why Miss Ellie would let us meet there. "*Yes.*"

"Is she just going to say yes to everything I ask?"

I punch a button. "*No.*"

I flick a quick look at his face. I don't know what the wide eyes and raised eyebrows mean but he looks like he's smiling a little, and smiles are supposed to be good, I think.

"Okay," he says. "Lottie, did you see what happened to Miss Ellie?"

"*Yes.*"

"What did you see?"

I swipe my finger, tap the buttons. "*Birds.*"

"Lottie . . . " Mom's voice has gone quiet, quiet and hard like a rock dropped in water. That voice when I don't do what she wants.

"Birds did something to Miss Ellie?" Detective Herring asks.

Of course the birds didn't do anything to Miss Ellie. But it's all connected, why can't he understand? I try to think, think of what prerecorded words I can use to tell him. To tell him about The Thing, The Thing that came down from the sky. Down from the sky and landed on the picnic table between us. I didn't look at it, not right at it, so I only saw it in bits, dark and fuzzy-edged like a storm cloud or a shadow. But it was solid and cold, and it made a sound like if a dog growled under water. And the birds all flew straight up and disappeared, up like fireworks until I couldn't see them in the sky. I'd never seen birds fly straight up like that. And The Thing took Miss Ellie and left. Took her but left her body. And Mom found me there, watching the sky, and Miss Ellie's body lying crumpled on the ground, her eyes and mouth open. I looked at her face, there on the ground. I usually don't like faces because they move too much, but Miss Ellie's face was still, and I didn't like that either.

"*Birds.*" I try again, then tap a few more words. "*Birds go. Miss Ellie go.*"

"Did you see any other people around her?"

This isn't working. I need to try something else. I look around and focus on the pictures in front of Detective Herring. A picture of Miss Ellie. A picture of the park and the picnic table. I reach across the table and pull them towards me. I glance around again and see a marker sticking out of Detective Herring's folder. I point at it, and he hands it to me. I take the lid off the marker and draw one big slashing line across Miss Ellie. Mom makes a little gasping sound like "Oh."

Then I take the picture of the picnic table and I try to draw The Thing. I try to draw it in black lines and fuzzy scribbles, there on the picnic table. And when I'm done, I make myself look at Detective Herring, and he's looking at me and I make my eyes look right in his eyes. After a second he nods. And I think maybe now they understand.

"Okay," he says. "Thank you, Lottie."

As we walk out of Detective Herring's building, Mom tucks my tablet back in her bag.

"You did a good job, Lottie," she says, and her voice is bright now, but a fake bright. Bright like a lightbulb, not like the sun. "Come on, let's go find some birds."

I look up at the sky. She didn't understand, after all. Did Detective Herring?

It's been three weeks since the birds disappeared. I wonder if they'll ever come back. But The Thing is still up there. Somehow, I know. Somehow, I feel it up there. And somehow, I'm pretty sure it *is* coming back.

***

The Future Adventures of Bailey Belvedere

THE FUTURE ADVENTURES OF BAILEY BELVEDERE:

As the societies of Earth collapse into chaos and destruction, Bailey Belvedere, a U.S. Army Intelligence officer fighting for her very survival, steals aboard an alien spacecraft, and soon finds herself given the authority and power by a superior alien entity to intervene in various problems in the Galaxy. Along the way she frees a world from interstellar slave traffickers, deals with an AI who becomes pregnant, inadvertently destroys a waffle house, fights against the abductors of a special child, and generally finds herself in some sort of trouble from one moment to the next.

Type: Novel – science fiction

Ordering Link:
Print Edition ($16.95):
https://www.hiraethsffh.com/product-page/further-adventures-of-bailey-belvedere-by-tyree-campbell

PDF Edition ($4.99):
https://www.hiraethsffh.com/product-page/further-adventures-of-bailey-belvedere-by-tyree-campbell-1

FOR 20% OFF, USE CODE BOOKS2025 WHEN YOU CHECK OUT!!!

River Valley Pawn
Heather Santo

"Where'd you get these?" Stanley picked up the Wilson Blade 104 v8 closest to him. He'd never played, but it was his business to know what things cost, and the punk across the counter had about a grand worth of tennis rackets.

Well, maybe "punk" was too strong a word. The kid appeared clean-cut, with brown hair and eyes. Early twenties, roughly five-foot nine. No visible scars, tattoos, or distinguishing features.

Still, after a lifetime in the pawn business, Stanley had a sixth sense for these things.

The kid shrugged. "Don't remember."

"You ain't the first forgetful person who's come in here, and you won't be the last." Stanley inspected the other rackets. All were in mint condition. "How about two-fifty for all four?"

The kid shifted uncomfortably.

"I could probably do three hundo." Stanley offered his hand. "Deal?"

"Actually," the kid lowered his voice and looked around to make sure no one else was in the shop, "I was hoping to trade for a phone call."

The pawn shop owner chuckled. *This* he hadn't expected.

"Yeah, we can trade for a phone call."

They shook hands. Stanley gathered up the rackets. He would tag and add them to the inventory later. "Follow me," he said, and walked around glass cases of jewelry, rows of firearms, and some furniture and electronics in one corner.

"Been here long?" the kid asked.

Stanley considered this. His grandfather had opened River Valley Pawn back in the late 1940s, and he'd basically grown up in the shop.

"A while."

Stanley stopped in front of three closed doors. The one on the far left led to the room where he slept. Inside was a narrow cot, microwave, and small dresser.

Stanley opened the middle door and placed the rackets on a stock room shelf.

Next, he removed a keyring from his pocket and unlocked the far-right door. Only a few people knew about this extension of the pawn shop. Stanley wondered how the kid had stumbled across the information.

He opened the door.

The room was dark and windowless. Leather bound books filled all available shelf space, and instead of jewelry, the display cases held ritual knives, bones, and teeth . . . some animal, some human. A scrying mirror. Pendulums, crystal balls, and spirit boards.

Stanley lit a candle and approached the center of the room. The tall, rectangular booth, made of glass and metal, looked out of place. *Never judge a book by its cover*, Stanley thought. Of all the things to cross the threshold of his shop, this was one of few that gave him nightmares.

A payphone, about as unremarkable as the kid standing next to him, hung in the booth.

He handed over two quarters.

"She's all yours."

The kid entered the booth. He inserted the coins, but his finger stopped short of the keypad. Like he was trying to recall a long-forgotten phone number.

Finally, he dialed and brought the receiver to his ear.

A shudder rattled Stanley's old bones. He'd only used the booth once.

He remembered the dull dial tone. The short bursts of sound as he punched in the phone number of his childhood home. The ringing of the other line.

Impossibly, someone had picked up.

At first, he'd only heard static. The scratchy noise prickled the skin on the back of his neck. Then a voice, muffled at first, but definitely trying to say something.

His name.

"S-s-stanley?" It was his younger sister. Her voice sounded echoey and far away, but still childlike. She'd been nine years old when she died.

"Amelia?" Tears fell, and emotion choked Stanley's throat.

"S-s-stanley, where are you?" his sister had cried.

"In Granddaddy's shop. Are you okay, Amelia? Where are you?"

She'd paused, and panic seized Stanley's heart.

"I walked through the f-f-fire. To a place beyond the f-f-flames."

A wave of nausea hit him. Twenty years prior, their house had caught fire in the middle of the night. Everyone escaped but their miniature poodle. Amelia had ripped free of their mother's arms and raced back inside.

Just then, Stanley had heard a familiar bark on the other end of the line.

"It's okay, S-s-stanley. Pierre is here. I f-f-found him."

He'd slammed the receiver down, just as the kid did now. Stanley said nothing, only watched as the kid walked briskly out of the room. A minute later, the bell on the front door jingled.

Stanley started to follow, but a deep growl, guttural, aggressive, somewhere between human and animal, caused him to turn. There was another door in the back of this room, and it rattled as something clawed at it from the other side.

Stanley backed away. This was the *other* thing that gave him nightmares. A thing that was always hungry. One he'd paid a steep price for. Not money, either.

A piece of his soul.

*

That night, a banging woke Stanley from restless sleep. He slipped from his room, and in the moonlight, saw the far-right door ajar. A tension wrench stuck out of the lock. Stanley slowly opened the stock room and pulled the closest object—the Wilson tennis racket—from a shelf. Gripping it in both hands, he crept into the back room.

A figure, dressed all in black, swept a flashlight beam around the space. Stanley swung the tennis racket, which made a dull thud as it connected with a skull. The intruder crumpled to the floor. Something else fell and clattered to one side.

A hand truck.

Stanley dropped the racket and picked up the flashlight. He shined it on the intruder's face.

"Knew you was a punk," the pawn shop owner muttered. "Trying to steal my payphone."

He dragged the kid's unconscious body to the back of the back room. To the other door, one that wasn't locked with a key.

Stanley whispered an incantation, and the door opened. He shoved the kid into the darkness, and toward the thing, blacker than darkness, beyond.

Achievable Goals
Jamie Lackey

Harlow sat down at the dusty dining room table and gave up. His family was dead, all snuffed out in a single tragic moment. His sister had demanded a ride on one of the new highspeed zeppelins, and their parents had been delighted to indulge her.

And it had crashed, killing everyone aboard.

He'd been away at school, sitting in class and counting the minutes till lunch. He hadn't even known till the next day.

And now he was home, on an extended leave of absence. He expected his mother to come in through the door, his sister to run down the stairs, his father to yell from his office.

But they were gone.

And all of their possessions needed to be categorized and organized and sorted and dealt with, and it was all just too much. He couldn't do it.

He'd throw himself in the river, and then it would be someone else's problem.

A detached part of his mind wondered if perhaps this was not the best time to be making such large decisions, but throwing himself in the river felt like such an achievable goal that his feet were moving before he could really give it much thought.

He paused to lock the door behind him, then paused to stare at the key in his hand. Throwing himself in the river with the key in his pocket and the door locked felt inconsiderate. He bent to tuck it under the welcome mat. Surely whoever had to deal with . . . everything . . . would find it there.

A small gray kitten bumped up against his ankle. "Oi!" she said in a tiny, cheerful voice. "Do you happen to have any chicken livers?"

Harlow blinked at her for a moment, thinking. There wasn't much food in the house at all. Some stale bread, moldy cheese, a couple of inedible casseroles that the neighbors had pressed into his hands. "I'm afraid I don't."

"Well, that's a solvable problem," the kitten said. "You look like you can afford a trip to the butcher."

"Well, yes," Harlow said. Money wasn't a problem, not with all of his family's savings falling to him, and with Mr. Gilbert buying out his mother's half of their law firm so that Harlow wouldn't have to trouble himself with it.

"Excellent," the kitten said. She gathered herself, then pounced, landing neatly on his shoulder since he was still bent over, fingers on the welcome mat. "You're not really leaving the key to our house there, are you? We don't want to be burgled."

"Our house?" Harlow asked, standing carefully. The kitten's claws shifted against his skin, but he managed to get upright without incident.

"It's cold at night and you're lonely. Me moving in will solve both of our problems! Everyone wins!" The kitten backed up her claim by leaning her warm, furry flank against his cheek and purring.

It was very soothing.

And buying chicken livers was just as achievable a goal as throwing himself in the river. "Yeah, okay," he said.

His mother and the university both had always had a firm "no pets" rule, but the kitten needed him. He couldn't turn her away.

"Do you have a name?" he asked as he walked toward the market district.

"Not yet!" the kitten said. "It felt inconsiderate to choose one without your input."

Harlow thought about it while he walked. The kitten kept on purring. "How about River?" he said. Her gray fur was the same color as the river in winter, and she'd stopped him from throwing himself into it.

The detached part of his mind was very glad of that last bit.

"I like it!"

Harlow's heart warmed at River's approval.

He bought chicken livers. He also bought a pillow for River to sleep on, some string for her to play with, and a load of groceries to be delivered to the house, since it was all too much to carry.

River hopped down from his shoulder, her tiny feet surprisingly loud against the floor, and set out to explore her new home.

Harlow dragged himself to his sister's room and started organizing her books into separate "keep," "sell," and "decide later" piles. But then he found her diary and started thumbing through it, which led to crying. He was so tired of not being able to achieve a single task without crying.

River bounded in with cobwebs on her whiskers. She climbed into his lap and flopped against him. His family was still gone, his grief still a huge, ungainly force that felt impossible to overcome. The house was still full of things that he didn't know what to do with. He was still adrift and directionless.

"When was the last time you ate?" River asked, her voice gentle.

"You just want to eat," Harlow said, wiping away tears.

"Food is important for both humans and cats," River said. "Everyone knows that."

Harlow put the diary on the "keep" pile and carried River down to the kitchen to cook some chicken livers and make a sandwich.

He put the livers on one of his mother's favorite dishes and placed that on the table.

River's table manners were not refined, but it was better than eating alone.

Harlow's mother had never approved of cat people, and he wondered if taking in a kitten was a betrayal. But River was right. He was alone, and the nights were cold. River's solution to those problems was a good one. And she'd been right about food, too. The sandwich did help.

He was afraid that his grief would never go away. That it would always be a part of him.

River finished her meal and licked his nose. Her tongue was warm and raspy, and he laughed.

He couldn't remember the last time he'd laughed.

Maybe, eventually, his grief wouldn't be the biggest part of him.

River curled up his lap, warm and purring and present. And for now, that was enough.

Gate
Jason Eisenmenger

Logan clicked the start button on the video. The footage was from a camcorder.

"Okay, so here's the deal on vampires." He said as he took a drag from his cigarette and reached down to flick the ashes into the can of soda in front of him. The handcuffs he was wearing clanked against the table as he did so.

"The old ones are the ones with all the power. They get crazy strong, and the venerable ones are almost god-like. They can take a lot more punishment, too. Some develop special powers depending on their bloodline. They are some scary muthas, but the young ones are the worst. They have to feed constantly and have no control over their hunger. They are not as strong as the old ones, but they can still rip a man's head off like you or me tearing a piece of paper."

The man shifted in his seat as the psychiatrist noted a series of runic tattoos going up the inside of his right forearm.

"Yeah, so the thing is you don't want to scrap with them hand- to-hand, though I seen a few boys try. This one guy, Pete, actually put a beat down on a young one once with a pair of silver gauntlets. Fucker got him though. When a man's starting to get winded, the vampires just keep coming. Stamina of the undead and all that."

"I thought you said before that silver was for werewolves," the doctor said.

"Yeah, the wolves *really* hate silver. But the vamps don't like it none either. Takes a while longer to regenerate from silver wounds."

"So how do you kill a vampire then?"

"Well, there are only a couple ways to be sure. You can decapitate them. You can stake them in the heart, but good luck getting that to work. And then there is the sun. Not that there is much of that around these days."

"There is no sun in this world you come from, Mr. Cane?"

"Not like it is here, brother. We have shorter days. It's always cold at night. We get some days where it is a sort of dusk for weeks. Hence why we are over- fucking-run with vampires."

"So how then do you deal with the vampires?"

"There are a lot of people that just say, fuck it and join the blood farms. I hear it's not so bad. You get three squares a day and are encouraged to reproduce. Won't ever find me on a blood farm, though. Vampires are not too fond of the sauce tainting their food supply. And I ain't ever givin' up the bottle. Only thing that gets me by."

"What about holy water and crucifixes?"

"You shitting me? I guess you been watching too many movies. There are *some* classic rules in place. Young ones can't cross running streams of water and all that, but a crucifix will only kill a vampire if he laughs himself to death. The other way is to join a pack if they will have you."

"A pack?"

"Yeah, werewolves." A few hunnerd years ago, some of the wolves got together and offered asylum to humans that were tired of being hunted and decided to take the fight back to the vamps. They looked for the biggest, baddest dudes to join up and then the wars started. You see, a wolf comes to maturity a lot faster than a vampire. The first couple of years, they are wild as can be, but with time, they learn to control themselves and if everything is even, a wolf usually gets the better of a vampire; unless it's an old one. Course, the vampires are pretty organized, too. They work in covens and there is always an old one leading. Course the covens are small compared to a pack and the older ones don't like to take orders. A coven leader is worth at least ten wolves. Sometimes, they just wait the wolves out. Vampires have the whole immortality thing going for them, but I say if you turn to dust when I cut your head off, you ain't immortal."

"So, you are saying you have seen werewolves too, Mr. Cane?"

"Look, doc. I don't expect you to understand. Your world is still bright and sunny. You don't know shit about survival. God only knows how long it will be before they come through."

"You believe in God?"

"It's a figure of speech. If there was a God, he left my world a long time ago. You just have those zealots like the Church of the Eclipse now."

"I would like to hear more about them."

"Maybe some other time, asshole."

"Very well." So, tell me how you came to be in our world, Mr. Cane."

"Like I already told you, we found a gate. We started to come through for provisions."

"Weapons?"

"Not so much. The food man. The food . . . pretty good."

"You're saying there is a shortage of food?"

"Let me just say, we ain't got no fucking pizza chains in my world. The food over there is pretty bland. You can just go down to the market and buy a pineapple, you fucking twit. Fuck this place, but you have great food, I'll give you that."

"I see. Where is this gate you speak of?"

The man shifted in his seat and put the remains of his cigarette into the can of soda in front of him.

"I can't tell you that, Doc. I have probably said enough to get me killed as it is."

*****

"There! That's when the power was cut." Agent Logan said, pointing at the screen.

Just then there was a flicker in the fluorescent lighting overhead. The power cut off, bathing the interview room in a hellish red glow of emergency lighting.

"The rest is kind of grainy; something weird with the cameras."

The remainder of the footage played without sound. What appeared to be a shadow splayed across the wall and Mr. Cane flung himself backwards and mouthed a scream. The footage ended.

"This is all we have," Logan said.

"What do you think he was saying? "Agent Remy asked.

"Been some conjecture. The experts say, he shouts, "witch," and then starts mumbling something indecipherable."

"How old is this tape?"

"1984."

"Okay, Logan. I admit, it's some weird shit, but why are you showing it to me? Certainly no one took this joker seriously?"

Logan smiled. "Because we found the gate."

The Hungry Forest
Stephen W. Chappell

"Follow me," she said, a glint in her eye and a tease in her smile. "I know a place."

He happily followed as the sounds of the fairground organ dwindled behind them. The path led over a wooden bridge—no more than planks, really—and towards the dark forest beyond.

"Why is it called 'The Hungry Forest,' I wonder?" he asked innocently.

She smiled slyly. "I wonder."

They had met at the carnival just hours ago, and he had taken an instant liking to the young lass. Her long locks captured his attention, and her soft eyes and natural glow ensnared his heart. Smitten at first sight, he could do naught but be with her.

They played the games and rode the rides, ate the candied apples and shared shy glances. She threw one to him over her shoulder as she led him deeper into the forest.

Her eyes reminded him of someone. Another girl he had met, he thought. Perhaps the one from yesterday. They also played the games and rode the rides. But that had ended badly. She had been too shy, and he had gotten too angry. Rejected and scorned, he would be satisfied, one way or another.

"You linger behind," she said playfully. Deeper into the woods, the forest was darker, and the trees packed closer together. Their limbs stretched across the trail as if reaching for an embrace. He imagined that it was he that the branches sought, an illusion enhanced by the mist that now rose around his ankles and hung in the air.

"The better to admire you," he replied, wondering if it would be the softness of her amorous touch or something else that would satisfy his cravings. He remembered the shape of her scornful, angry lips and the cry that escaped them at his touch. He thought of the blood that flowed over his hands as he plunged them into her chest. He savored the memory of her warm, still-beating heart as he caressed it.

"Well, then, perhaps we should rest here." An old oak spread its branches invitingly around them as the mist climbed higher. A dark, gaping hollow marred its sturdy trunk, as did the trees to either side. He wondered briefly at the sort of creature that might inhabit such a place. But she showed no worry as she leaned against the mighty oak and tilted her head back expectantly.

A wolfish smile played ever so briefly across his lips. He approached her and leaned in for a kiss. Behind him, the branches of the oak reached down as if to shield them from the eyes of curious passersby.

She stopped him with a finger to his lips. "Not yet." She caressed his cheek as the darkness closed in on them. Entranced by her brilliant gaze, he could see only her soft, beautiful face and the intensity of her dazzling green eyes.

The trees creaked and groaned as if swaying in a storm. The thrill of her touch, slight though it had been, drew such attention from him that he had none left to observe that he had felt not the slightest breeze.

"Tell me of the others," she said breathlessly.

His breath caught in his throat. "There are no others," he lied. "Only you, my first love." A chill traveled the length of his spine as something brushed past his arm. He pasted on an unconvincing smile and leaned closer.

She smiled knowingly, an unyielding hand pressed firmly on his chest. "But what of the girl last night?" Her smile grew menacing as a fire grew in her eyes. "What lie did you tell her?" She lowered her voice to a whisper. "Do you even remember her name?"

The pretense fell from his face as his heart hardened and his fingers flexed. In truth, he preferred the satisfaction that came from blood rather than the softer variety. A sneer twisted his features as he leaned ever closer. "I don't even know yours."

He shifted uncomfortably as leaves whipped about his feet. He lifted his arms towards her, clawed hands reaching for her delicate throat.

Something rough wrapped around his right arm. He yanked, but it was held fast. He moved his left hand towards it, but an iron-hard branch stretched across its path and twisted around his bicep. A falling leaf kissed his cheek as the branches pulled and he struggled against them.

"I know what you did last night." Her playful, promising mask slipped away to reveal hatred hidden beneath. "She was my *sister*."

His eyes flew wide as branches wrapped around his waist, first from one side, then the other.

"It is ok, you poor boy," she said as she stepped aside to reveal the gaping maw behind her. The tree's dark hollow smiled at him. Long, jagged teeth gnashed within it. To either side, the menacing oaks moved closer. "The trees are hungry. And they eat meat."

Who?

Vincent Baverso holds a degree from the University of Pittsburgh in English writing. By day, he drafts architectural plans, by night he immerses himself in mead making, philosophy, art, fashion, cobbling, horology, and many other forms of tinkering. His creative versatility spans from carpentry to canvas, but his true love lies in the written word, with works published in several anthologies and journals for both poetry and science fiction. He is the author of the haiku collection *The 49 Stalks* and is always putting words on paper. When not pursuing his latest project, he enjoys life with his wife and three children. Learn more at his website www.vbaverso.com

Amanda Bergloff is a digital/mixed media artist of the weirder things in life. Her cover art has been published by the Jules Verne Society's *Extraordinary Visions Anthology, Utopia Science Fiction, Fear Forge, The Horror Zine,* and others. She lives in Denver, Colorado, and is a shameless collector of over 4,000 horror paperbacks, along with vintage toys and comics. Follow her on X @AmandaBergloff

Maureen Bowden is a Liverpudlian, living with her musician husband in North Wales. She has had 210 stories and poems accepted by paying markets including *Third Flatiron, Water Dragon Publishing, The First Line*, and many others. She was nominated for the 2015 international Pushcart Prize and in 2019 Hiraeth Books published an anthology of her stories, *Whispers of Magic*. They plan to publish an anthology of her poetry in the near future. She also writes song lyrics, mostly comic political satire, set to traditional melodies and her husband has performed them in folk music clubs throughout the UK. She loves her family and friends, rock 'n' roll, Shakespeare, and cats.

S.D. Bullard: Welcome to my crazy life. It's filled with chaos and words, an unusual and demanding day job, the act of single parenting, the most fabulous 10-year-old twins who came to me via adoption from foster care, and too many dogs (subsequently too much dog hair). We've settled our little tornado in Middle Tennessee for the time, where I conquer the demands of the day (who am I kidding: I just survive them), then cram writing time into the late hours of the night and early hours of the morning.

Steve Chappell is the chosen servant of four feline overlords who grudgingly tolerate his service. They live in the outskirts of the NJ pine barrens with his wife. He currently works as a systems engineer. His stories have appeared in previous issues of *Flash*

Digest and in *Dark Horses Magazine*, as well as in several anthologies, including *Ruth and Ann's Guide to Time Travel* and *Deadly Flames: Dragons in Combat*. Besides writing, he enjoys reading, photography, and hiking. He can be found on BlueSky at @swchappell.bsky.social.

Tom Duke lives in the foothills west of the Palomar Mountain Observatory (Hale telescope) with his wife, Michelle, two strange dogs, and a furry gray demon who thinks she's a cat. He also writes poetry, songs and guitar instrumentals.

Jason Eisenmenger was born in Dallas, TX. He received his MA in Literature from Texas State University and is currently a professor of composition and literary studies at Austin Community College. Jason enjoys fantasy literature and games as well as travel and singing. He lives in Austin with his wife, Samantha, and two dogs: Bill Murray and Miles.

Jamie Lackey lives in Pittsburgh with her husband and their cats. She has had over 200 short stories published in places like *Beneath Ceaseless Skies, Apex Magazine*, and *Escape Pod*. She has a novella and two short story collections available from Air and Nothingness Press, and she's created six successful crowdfunding campaigns to self-publish a novel, two novellas, a novelette, and three short story collections. In addition to writing, she spends her time reading, playing tabletop RPGs, baking, mushroom hunting, and hiking. You can find her online at www.jamielackey.com.

Heather Santo is a category manager living in Pittsburgh, PA with her husband and two children. In addition to writing, her interests include photography, travel, and collecting skeleton keys. Follow her on Instagram and X @Heather52384.

Richard E Schell works in the biomedical field in California. He enjoys writing and has published over 100 articles and other works in both the biomedical field as well as in fictional genres and poetry. He enjoys photography, literature and travel. He also volunteers in animal rescue.

END OF TRANSMISSION

www.ingramcontent.com/pod-product-compliance
Lightning Source LLC
LaVergne TN
LVHW021953060526
838201LV00049B/1686